LITTLE DOG

by Lisa Jahn-Clough

Houghton Mifflin Company Boston 2006

Walter Lorraine Books

for Happy

thanks to Mom

Walter Lorraine *wL* Books

www.houghtonmifflinbooks.com

Library of Congress Cataloging-in-Publication Data
Jahn-Clough, Lisa.
    Little Dog / by Lisa Jahn-Clough.
        p. cm.
    Summary: A lonely stray dog befriends a struggling artist,
transforming her art and both their lives.
    ISBN-13: 978-0-618-57405-6
    ISBN-10: 0-618-57405-0
[1. Dogs—Fiction. 2. Artists—Fiction.] I. Title.
    PZ7.J153536Lit 2006
    [E]—dc22
                                            2005020455

Manufactured in China
SCP 10 9 8 7 6 5 4 3 2 1

Little Dog lived on the streets.

Little Dog was hungry. He was tired.
He wanted to eat and sleep and chase things.

Most of all, he wanted someone to love.

Little Dog roamed the city.
Everyone told him to scram.

It was a hard life, but
Little Dog kept hoping.

8

One day there was a big festival.
No one noticed Little Dog.

Little Dog slipped into a building.
In the back someone was hanging a painting.

Rosa was an artist.
Her paintings were sad and dark.

Little Dog took a chance and rolled on Rosa's feet.

"A little dog!" Rosa said. "Want some food?"
Little Dog's tail went thump, thump, thump.

"You're so scruffy. You're so scrappy,"
Rosa said. "But you're so happy."
Little Dog's tail thumped faster.
"You can stay," said Rosa.

Rosa gave Little Dog a sudsy bath and
made him a cozy place to sleep.

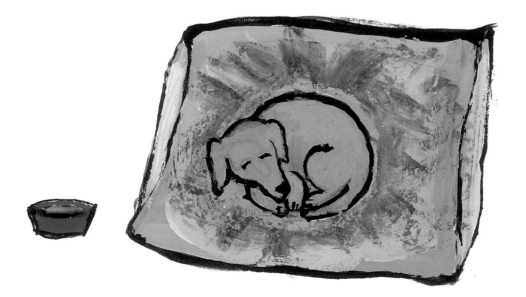

In the morning Rosa and Little Dog went out.
Rosa started to paint with her usual dark colors.
Little Dog pranced around.
"This doesn't feel right," Rosa said.

"I don't want to paint these
gloomy pictures anymore."
Little Dog wriggled with joy.

"What can I do?" cried Rosa.

Little Dog woofed and yipped and wagged his tail.

"Where are you going, Little Dog? Wait for me!"

Rosa followed Little Dog a long way.
The city buildings changed to houses
and then to hills with trees and flowers.

They were in the country!

Little Dog took a deep breath.
The air smelled of fresh grass and
lots of creatures to chase.

Rosa took out her paints.
The world was full of color
and growing things.

Little Dog frolicked and Rosa painted.
When the sun began to set they packed up.
"What a beautiful day this has been," Rosa said.
Little Dog yipped in delight.

When they got back to the city
everything looked different.
Little Dog played while Rosa
painted and painted and painted.

Finally Rosa hung up her new paintings.

Everyone admired Rosa's art.
"So bright! So cheerful!" they said.

"Thank you," Rosa said.
"I could not have done it without Little Dog."

Little Dog looked at the paintings.
He was in every one.

Little Dog jumped into Rosa's arms.
"I'm so happy you found me," said Rosa.
Little Dog was happy, too.

Epilogue

Rosa and Little Dog moved to the country.
Rosa had plenty of colorful things to paint.
Little Dog had plenty of food to eat, time to nap,
creatures to chase, and lots of love.